For Mum and Dad and my three little chickadees:
Rebecca, Brendan, and Ian —M. A.

To my big sis, Deb —S. McG

Clarion Books
3 Park Avenue
New York, New York 10016

Clarion Books is an imprint of Houghton Mifflin Harcourt Publishing Company.
www.hmhco.com

Library of Congress Cataloging-in-Publication Data is available.
ISBN 978-1-328-66081-7

Manufactured in China
SCP 10 9 8 7 6 5 4 3 2 1
4500658179

Marie Alafaci

Illustrated by Shane McG

ZELDA'S
BIG ADVENTURE

CLARION BOOKS

Houghton Mifflin Harcourt

Boston   New York

Zelda had a plan.
She was going to be
the first chicken in space.

She built her spaceship.
She planned her experiments.

3/4 + 2x 4/6 =
3 cups of
moondust

She trained for weightlessness.
All she really needed now was
a little help from her friends.

So she asked Walter for help with her spacesuit.
"Certainly not!" said Walter. "I don't sew!"

Then she asked Mike for help with her heat shields. "No time," said Mike. "No time."

Then she asked Bella for help with the controls.
"My dear Zelda," said Bella, "I don't do DIY."
Zelda was stumped.
How was she going to be the first chicken
in space if no one was willing to help her?

"Well," she said to herself
after a good, long think,
"I'll just have to manage all on my own."
So she did.

Finally, launch day arrived.
Zelda checked her fuel tank—full.
She checked her food bowl—bursting.
She checked her nesting box—cozy.

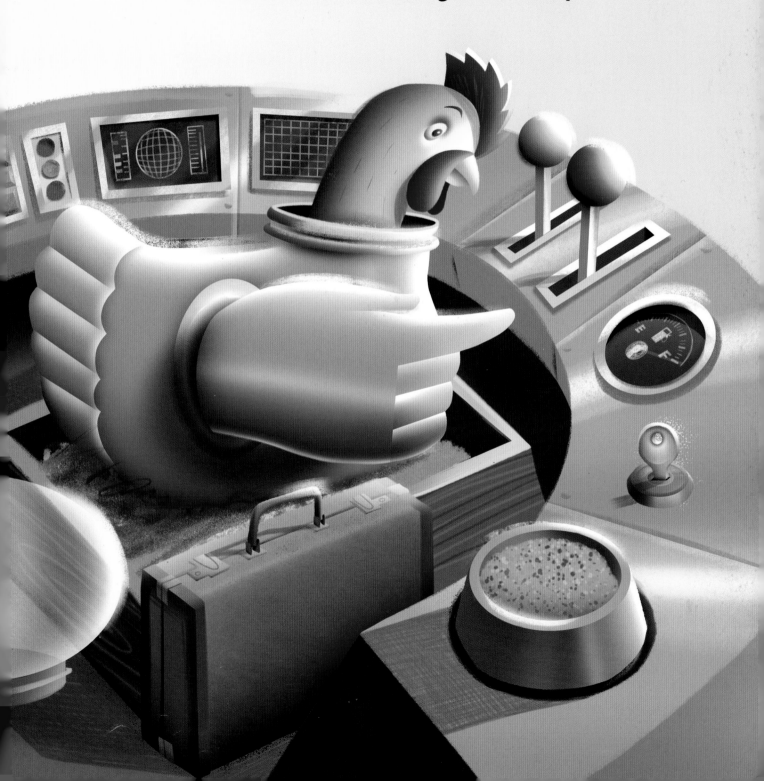

Zelda started
her engine...
"Ten...
three...
eight...
um...
four..."
—she wasn't very good
at counting backwards—
"zero...
BLAST OFF!"
she cried.

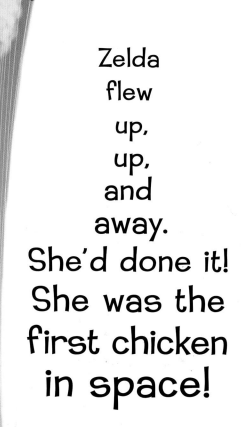

Zelda
flew
up,
up,
and
away.
She'd done it!
She was the
first chicken
in space!

Zelda conducted her experiments
and went on spacewalks.
She weighed stardust and counted planets.
It was hard work, but she managed
all on her own.

When Zelda came home,
everyone wanted to hear
about her amazing adventure.

"Strictly between us," said Walter,
"she asked me to work
on her spacesuit.
She looks rather fine,
doesn't she?"

"I'm not one to brag," said Mike,
"but she asked me to
fine-tune her heat shields.
I like to keep warm, you see."

"Just confidentially," said Bella,
"she asked me to tweak
her control panel.
I have a mind for
electronics, you know."

Everyone agreed it was by far
the most interesting thing that had
ever happened in their yard.

Later that night, before she closed her eyes,
Zelda looked up at the stars one more time.
They seemed smaller from down here,
but just as beautiful, and Zelda felt proud
to have been on such a big adventure.

"Space travel is fun," she said to herself,
"but it is rather lonely...

"Perhaps I'll
bring some friends
next time."